Frederick Xcalibur

by
Kathy
Boltz
Phillips

Frederick Xcalibur

Written and Illustrated by
Kathy Boltz Phillips

Dedication
I dedicate this book to all the little children coming into this world that want and need guidance to be the best person they can be. Everyone is given a talent and if this talent is used to help others, one's life is fulfilled and happy.

Acknowledgments
I thank Linda Margetin, Wendy Osthaus, and my husband Richard Filipiak for helping to edit the story.

Kathy Boltz Phillips
LeisureTimeArt L.L.C.
2745 Lari Court
West Bloomfield, MI 48324
248 683 8848
Email: kbpartist@leisuretimeart.com   Web: leisuretimeart.com

Published by Comet Publishing
U.S.A.

Produced by David Kinder
Burton Printing Company/Comet Publishing
4270 S. Saginaw St.
Burton, Mi 48529
{810} 742- 3210
Email: burtonprinting@sbcglobal.net

Printed in Hong Kong
Library of Congress Cataloging-in-Publication Data on file.
ISBN: 978-0-9753741-4-6

Frederick Xcalibur was a dragon who lived a long, long time ago. He was your typical dragon, always going around burning villages with his dragon breath and robbing the villagers of their food. His favorite sporting event was to fight other dragons for superiority. Therefore, Frederick was bruised and hurting all the time.

One day Frederick landed in a village with full intentions of stealing something to eat. To his surprise the villagers had wised up and hid all their food. Frederick couldn't find a morsel anywhere.

A nice little boy named Nelson wandered into the path of the dragon and introduced himself. "Hi there dragon. I'm Nelson. What's your name?"

"My name is Frederick Xcalibur," said Frederick.
"You don't look so good," said Nelson. "What's wrong?"

"I'm starving," Frederick wailed. "I'm tired of fighting,
and my fire breath is broken. I don't know what to do."

Nelson thought for a moment. "Your present lifestyle isn't working for you. Why don't you work for your food instead of stealing it all the time? Look at you, you're all beaten up, your throat flame has gone out, and you're depressed. You need a change."

"Now, the first thing we have to do is clean you up", said Nelson. "I will get some medicine to help heal up these cuts and bruises. You can't go for a job looking like a thug."

"The next thing we will do is get you some food", said Nelson.

"Then we will have to get you some honey and spicy hot, hot chili for that throat. The honey will make your throat better and the spicy hot, hot chili will turn on your fire breath. That should make you feel better".

Frederick asked, "Nelson, what do you mean by a job?
Just what do you think I'm capable of doing?"

Nelson replied, "You are capable of doing anything you want.
What do you really like to do? What do you think about all
the time that makes you happy?"

"Hmmmmmm," thought Frederick. "I really like to use my fire breathing ability."

"Okay, now what do you think you can do with that ability to help others in some way?" asked Nelson.

"Well, I could keep the night lamps lit in the village all night long."
"Frederick, that's a great idea. Now you're thinking."
"But Nelson, how does that get me some food?"
"Frederick, the people of the village will hire you to do that good deed and they can pay you with food."
Frederick smiled and said, "I'm starting to feel better all ready."

"Is there anything else you really like to do?" said Nelson.
"My real passion is flying," said Frederick. "There is nothing better than being able to get from one place to another really fast."
"So Frederick, how would your flying help others?"

"I could fly people, food and supplies from one village to another." Nelson smiled and said "Frederick, that's a wonderful idea. I'll bet villagers would be so happy, that they would pay you with enough food so you would never have to steal or fight again."
"But Nelson," said Frederick, "I'm a ferocious, fire breathing dragon. Won't the villagers be afraid of me?"

"Frederick, if you want to do these things, I will help you. I will be your first passenger to go on a flight to show the villagers you're not dangerous. Then we can take some supplies to another village to show them how fast you can deliver goods from one village to another.

The villagers will pay you because you will be very helpful to them," exclaimed Nelson.

Frederick Xcalibur is Kathy's second children's book. Frederick Xcalibur is a dragon character that was created and designed by Kathy. Being an artist, she illustrated the dragon and modeled him into all different poses and she wrote this story imagining the dragon with a little boy. In the first book, The Day the Electricity Went Out, the story was about teaching children how to go outside and play. Within this new book the message is that you must go out and work for what you want, not just take it. Kathy is trying to show children how to listen to their hearts and use their passion to benefit them self and others. It's a colorful depiction of classic bad dragon behavior turning to good with a message of helping others.

Kathy Boltz Phillips is a watercolor artist originally from Johnstown, PA. She now resides in West Bloomfield, MI. She has a Bachelor of Science degree from Indiana University of Pennsylvania. She taught music in middle school for four years then started a family. She also started taking painting lessons one night a week. That's when she laid down her clarinet, picked up a paint brush and never looked back.

Kathy has been painting in watercolor for 35 years and is a recognized professional artist selling her watercolor paintings at fine art fairs and galleries in several states. She teaches art classes in West Bloomfield and also is an instructor for the Society of Decorative Painters. Kathy has taught at art conventions in Las Vegas NV, Columbus OH, Providence RI, the Poconos PA, Lansing MI, and Canada. Her experience with presentations and demonstrations during these classes has become an inspiration for many others because of her unique talent and creativity.

Visit Kathy's website: LeisureTimeArt.com
Email address: kbpartist@leisuretimeart.com